My p Sound Box

by Jane Belk Moncure

illustrated by Linda Sommers

THE CHILD'S WORLD

MANKATO, MN 56001

Library of Congress Cataloging in Publication Data

Moncure, Jane Belk.
  My p sound box.

  (Sound box books)
  SUMMARY: A little girl fills her sound box with
many words that begin with the letter "p."
  [1. Alphabet]   I. Sommers, Linda.   II. Title.
III. Series.
PZ7.M739Myp   [E]   78-7841
ISBN 0-89565-047-9 -1991 Edition

My ''p'' Sound Box

(Blends are included in this book.)

Little  had a box.

"I will find things that begin with my 'p' sound," she said.

"I will put them into my sound  ."

Little  found a poodle

and her puppy.

Did she put the poodle and puppy into the box?

She did.

Then Little p found a   pig

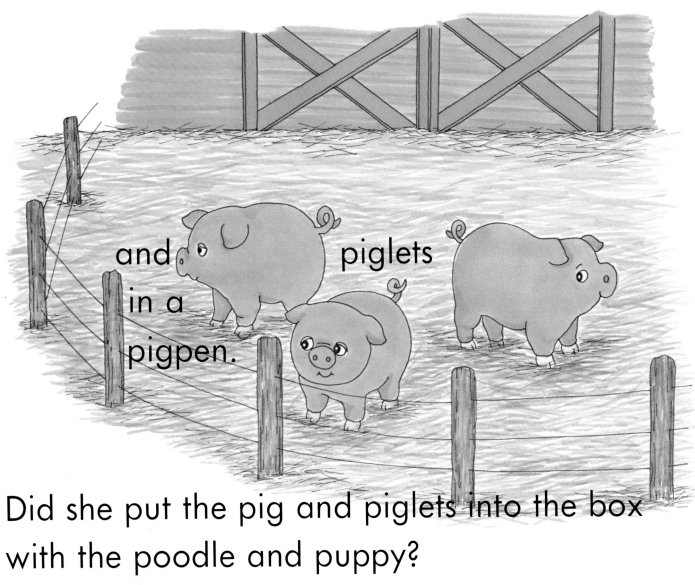

and piglets in a pigpen.

Did she put the pig and piglets into the box with the poodle and puppy?
She did.

Little P walked down a path to the PARK.

In the park, she saw a tree with peaches.
She put some peaches
into her box.

Under the
peach tree, Little

saw a picnic table and a picnic basket.

"Let's have a picnic," said Little p. She opened the picnic basket and found peanuts, pickles, popcorn, and pie.

Little p and the animals

ate until the pig said,

"I am about to pop!"

So Little p put the animals back into the box.

She also put back the leftover peanuts, pickles, popcorn, and pie.

Now the box was so heavy, it was about to pop!

Then Little  P saw a

pony pulling a pink cart.

"Please pull us!" she said.

The pony pulled them down the path.

They saw a

porcupine.

Little P gave the porcupine
some popcorn.

She put him into the box ... carefully ...
because he was prickly.

The pony pulled them on down the path.

Soon they saw a peacock.

Little **P** gave the peacock some peanuts.

Then she put him into the box.

Suddenly the pony stopped.

A panther

was in the path!

The pony pranced!
The pig, piglets, poodle, puppy, peacock, and porcupine fell out of the box.

The panther pounced on the box.

He ate up all the peanuts,
pickles, peaches, popcorn, and pie!

Then he smiled politely!

Just then, a policeman

came down the path.

"You have found our pet panther," he said.
"We will take him back to the zoo."

"Let's take all of my pets to the petting zoo,"

said Little P.

25

piglet

picnic basket

porcupine

pony

park

piglet

piglet

pig

puppy

They had a parade

peaches

policeman

peacock

poodle

path

panther

all the way to the petting zoo.

Can you read these words with Little  ?

pretzel

panda

pencil

PASTE

parrot

plane

pelican

parachute

puppet

plate

penguin

pocket

piano